# BUNDLES OF JOY

**Tianamonet Tobie**
**Edited by: Tianamonet Tobie**

To order additional copies of this book, contact:
Xlibris
844-714-8691
www.Xlibris.com
Orders@Xlibris.com

ISBN:    Softcover      978-1-6641-3384-6
         EBook          978-1-6641-3383-9

Library of Congress Control Number: 2020919091

Print information available on the last page

Rev. date: 05/31/2023

# BUNDLES OF JOY

To all the mommy's and daddy's, love your children for they're the future! Protect your children for they're your shinning Stars! Support your children for they're your Super Heros! Invest in your children for they're your success! Admire your children, because they admire you! Spend time with your children, because they cherish spending time with you! Play with your children, because quality time is the best time! Read with your children, because bonding is essential! Run around the park, and be a big kid with your children, because laughter and happiness is healthy! Pray with your children always before eating, because it's a blessing to be fortunate! Praise GOD every night with your children for they always pray for you! Give hugs, kisses, belly rubs, back rubs, and unconditional love to your children, because one day you'll be old, and they'll return all of this effort back to you!

I dedicate this book to my twelve year old son, Dai'Jon Pryor and my ten year old daughter, Kah'Lonee' Pryor! I love you both so much with all of my heart, mind, and soul mommy prince and princess!

# Table of Contents

# BUBBLE BATH TIME

Princess:
Can I please take a bath Mommy? It would really mean a lot to me if I can play with all of my new toys in the water!

Mommy:
I'll think about it daughter. . .

Princess:
I love taking a bubble bath, it's so much fun! Pretty please, let me take a bubble bath Mommy, it would make me so happy!

Mommy:
Later my mini me Princess.

Princess:
How come it has to be later Mommy?

Mommy:
You have to eat your healthy snack, and clean up your room for Mommy!

Princess:
But Mommy. . .

Mommy:
Yes beautiful?

Princess:
If I take a bath now all of the bubbles will put me to sleep! Don't you want me to take a nap Mommy? Isn't that how I grow to be strong like you?

Mommy:
OK, Mommy will let you take your bubble bath now, and play with your new toys! When you wake up from your nap, you have to eat your healthy snack, floss, brush your teeth, mouthwash then clean up your room for Mommy!

Princess:
Yes Mommy, but can you please read me a story while I play with my toys in the water?

Mommy:
Of course my mini me, it's a deal!

Princess:
I love you so much Mommy!

Mommy:
I love you so much more Mommy Princess!

They both smiled as Mommy hugged her daughter Kah'Lonee' tightly, and gave her a kiss on her cheek!

The end!

# PARK HOPPING DAY

Prince:
Can we go park hopping today, and bring our bikes, scooters, cars, and skates Mom?

Mom:
What did I tell you yesterday before you went to school son?

Prince:
You told me we'll go park hopping today after school if I do my homework!

Mom:
What else?

Prince:
And if I pick up my toys from on my bedroom floor, so you can vacuum.

Mom:
What else?

Prince:
Oh! If I organize my backpack!

Mom:
Keep going son!

Prince:
That's it Mom! What else can there be on the list?

Mom:
Keep trying to figure it out!

Mom and son laughed as she begin to boil his green veggies, and make his fruit salad!

Mom:
So, have anything else came to my son mind?

Prince:
I got it! You want me to take a shower, floss, brush my teeth, and mouthwash, because I've been at school all day!

Mom:
I do want you to floss, brush your teeth, and mouthwash before we leave out, but if we're going to the park, than you'll shower afterwards.

Prince:
It's healthy snack time. . .

Mom:
That's right son, but you already knew that!

Prince:
I did, but my fingers are still crossed under the table!

Mom:
That's a funny one!

Prince:
I can't stop laughing!

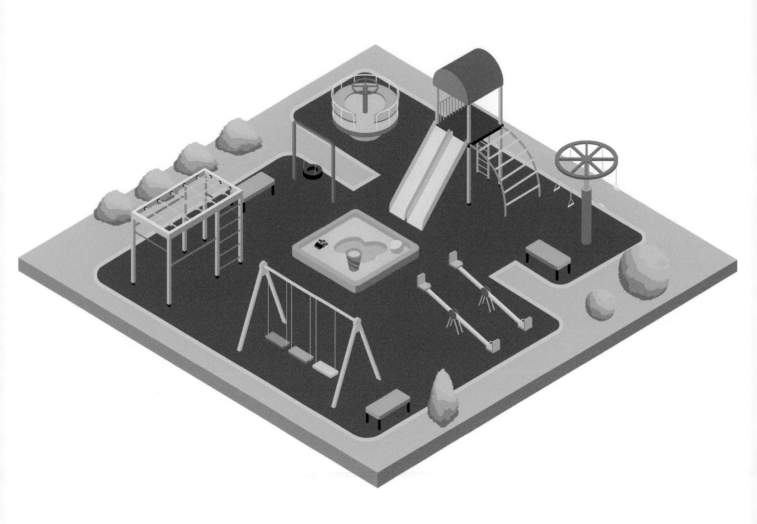

Mom:
I love you Mommy big boy Prince!

Prince:
I love you more Mom!

Mom gave her son Dai'Jon a tight hug, and a kiss on his cheek as they both smiled!

The end!

# FUN DAY

Happy Thanksgiving

Our bags are all packed for Thanksgiving break, and we're ready to go have lots of fun!

(Day 1)
We had so much fun at story time with reading lots of books, made some very cool drawings, baked cookies together, enjoyed making creative characters with finger painting, and played some exciting board games!

(Day 2)
We rode our bikes outside, played at a huge park, skated around our community, and had a picnic in our backyard!

(Day 3)
We made breakfast together, played some card games, made lunch together, played on some very cool game consoles, made dinner together, and had a great movie night with some popcorn, and a healthy snack!

(Day 4)

We checked our bags to make sure we were complete, gathered plenty of cold water bottles, snacks, and sandwiches. While on our road trip we enjoyed looking out the window, telling jokes, sharing laughs, conversations, and playing lots of car games!

(Day 5)
We arrived at two of our favorite water parks, and got on tons of water slides! We also went surfing, swimming in the lazy pool, and swimming in the wave pool.

AMUSEMENT PARK

TICKETS

(Day 6)
We arrived at one of our favorite amusement parks; got on all of the roller coasters, and other fun rides too!

(Day 7)
We arrived at our second favorite amusement park; got on all of the roller coaster rides before it was time to drive back to the hotel to take a shower, pack our bags, and travel back to our home sweet home!

The end!

# LOVE YOUR NEIGHBOR

He is small, and short.
He is white with brown spots.
He is fury, and cute.
He is nice, but shy.

He is one of a kind, and funny.
He is old, but act young.
He is very alert, and smart.
He is funny, and quiet.

He walks on four legs, and is quick.
He loves to groom himself, and be rubbed.
He loves taken long walks, and going swimming.
He barks when he is hungry, or thirsty.

He does the running man when he needs to go outside. He is active, and a great companion. He was born on May 31, 2000. He is Tianamonet Tobie twenty year old Chihuahua name Poppee Pryor Tobie, who she has been raising in her loving home since he was two years old!

The end!

# DREAMS

Can I dream big daddy?

How big can I dream?

Can I be who I want to be daddy?

How can I make my dreams come true?

I want to sing like a bright shining star!
I want to dance like the clouds in the sky!
I want to be a great Gymnastic Super Star!
I want to make people happy by laughing, and smiling!

I want to learn like an open book!
I want to live big like a huge heart that lights up!
I want to shine so bright like a diamond that sparkles!
I want to bring a glow to the world like the sun!

Dream big!

I am so proud to hear how you have such big dreams daughter!

Tell me what are your dreams son?

I want to be a great Artist, Author, and Gamer, so the world will know my name dad!

If the world know my name, they will know who I am, where I come from, when I was born, and why I was born!

I am so proud to hear how you have such big dreams son!

I am such a proud father with faith, and belief! I love you both so much, and I am honored to have you both as my son, and my daughter! I know you both will move mountains, and make great changes! You both can be who you want to be, and want to be who you become!

You both can dream as big as you will allow yourself! I am sure all of your dreams will come true for the both of you, if you remain true to your dreams, and never give up! Just remember how some people are dreamers, and some people have dreams!

The end!

Printed in the United States
by Baker & Taylor Publisher Services